COMICS SQUAD

LUNCH!

★ COMICS BY ★

CECE BELL

JEFFREY BROWN

CECIL CASTELLUCCI & SARA VARON

NATHAN HALE

JENNIFER L. HOLM & MATTHEW HOLM

JARRETT J. KROSOCZKA

PEANUTS

JASON SHIGA

COMICS SQUAD
SQUAD
LUNCH!

· EDITED BY ·

JENNIFER L. HOLM, MATTHEW HOLM &
JARRETT J. KROSOCZKA

Fortified with eight essential vitamins!

WAIT—WE DON'T HAVE TO **EAT** THE BOOK, DO WE?

RANDOM HOUSE 🏠 NEW YORK

FOR EVA, ROBIN, AND SCOTT— COMICS SQUAD SUPERHEROES!

They're scrumptious!

Compilation copyright © 2016 by Jennifer L. Holm, Matthew Holm, and Jarrett J. Krosoczka

"Crazy Little Thing Called Lunch!" copyright © 2016 by Cece Bell. "Snoopy in . . . Lunchtime Beagle" copyright © 2016 by Peanuts Worldwide LLC. "Babymouse: Lunch Table Champion" copyright © 2016 by Jennifer L. Holm and Matthew Holm. "The Case of the Missing Science Project" copyright © 2016 by Jason Shiga. "Pikput & Cullen in . . . Worst Day Ever!" copyright © 2016 by Cecil Castellucci and Sara Varon. "Lucy & Andy Neanderthal: Cave Soup" copyright © 2016 by Jeffrey Brown. "Lunch Bomb 1943" copyright © 2016 by Nathan Hale. "Lunch Girl and the Ominous Origin" copyright © 2016 by Jarrett J. Krosoczka.

Cover art copyright © 2016 by Jennifer L. Holm and Matthew Holm, Jarrett J. Krosoczka, Cecil Castellucci and Sara Varon, Cece Bell, Jason Shiga, Nathan Hale, Jeffrey Brown, and Peanuts Worldwide LLC

All rights reserved. Published in the United States by Random House Children's Books, a division of Penguin Random House LLC, New York.

Random House and the colophon are registered trademarks of Penguin Random House LLC.

Visit us on the Web! randomhousekids.com

Educators and librarians, for a variety of teaching tools, visit us at RHTeachersLibrarians.com

Library of Congress Cataloging-in-Publication Data is available upon request.

ISBN 978-0-553-51264-9 (trade) — ISBN 978-0-553-51265-6 (lib. bdg.) — ISBN 978-0-553-51266-3 (ebook)

MANUFACTURED IN CHINA

10 9 8 7 6 5 4 3 2 1

First Edition

Random House Children's Books supports the First Amendment and celebrates the right to read.

★ CONTENTS ★

I'M STARVING! CAN WE EAT LUNCH YET?

Well, what are we waiting for?!

I pack my own lunch every day. And every day, I eat *exactly* the same things. No matter *what*.

Little Betty® nut-free double oatmeal cookie with white "creme" in the middle

Bologna sandwich on brown bread, mustard ONLY!

Chester Cow™ chocolate milk (6 oz.)

medium-sized Granny Smith apple

3 baby carrots (one is in my mouth right now)

Hey, Ellie, you should try some of this pizza boat! It's good!

Um...uh...

I *like* having the same thing to eat every day. I mean, what if I change my lunch, and **crazy** things start happening? I know it's not that simple, but—*what if?*

...uh... no thanks?

Better safe than sorry...

Psst...let's move to another table. Ellie is *weird!*

Hmm. There's Franklin from Spanish class. He's so cute. Is he *juggling*? Wow.

The only thing that guy *can't* do is notice *me*. That's OK—I can notice *him!*

Uh, excuse me—

4

Um...hi, Ellie!

Franklin? Talking? To me?

Well, you see, I'm selling these candy bars for drama club and I

So dreamy...

Wanna buy one?

Oh *no!* A candy bar is *not* part of my lunch! There's no way I can eat *that!*

Um...er...

But it's Franklin! And I don't actually have to eat it, right?

Well?

YES! I'll do it! I mean— ahem—I'll buy one!

That'll be one dollar, please!

5

6

But—but—you've turned into *my bologna sandwich!*

BA-*LONEY!*

No, *really!*

That's OK. No one else seems to notice, so—

Que será, será!*

*"Whatever will be, will be" in Spanish. It's on the test today!

But *yuck!* You should *totally* be using mayo instead of mustard!

Hee hee! Is he *seriously* OK with this?

I don't know *what* is happening—but if Franklin can be this cool about being a bologna sandwich, then maybe I can be cool about eating even more of this candy bar....

Hey, you know what?

I'm gonna go get my lunch and eat with you. You're kinda funny!

Franklin. Is gonna eat lunch with *me.* He might be a bologna sandwich, but he's still Franklin!

15 seconds later...

Ugh. Peanut butter. I'll trade ya it for your Little Betty cookie....

That's one thing I *know* I shouldn't try. The last time I had nuts, I got a little bit dizzy.

Uh...

17 minutes later...

Where *am* I?

Ellie? Are you OK? Oh my gosh, you took *one bite* of that candy bar and then you *passed out!*

You kept mumbling *que será, será* and *bologna* and all kinds of stuff!

He's not a bologna sandwich anymore. *Huh!*

I'm OK, I think....

Very OK!

Whew! Well, here's your stuff. I'll carry it to Spanish for you.

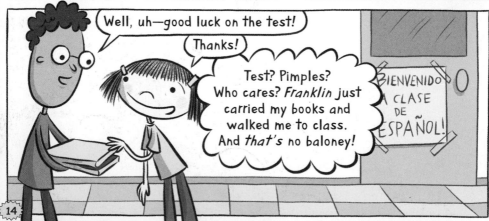

Well, uh—good luck on the test!

Thanks!

Test? Pimples? Who cares? *Franklin* just carried my books and walked me to class. And *that's* no baloney!

BIENVENIDO A CLASE DE ESPAÑOL!

The next day, I pack my lunch like I always do...

but this time, I put mayo on my sandwich instead of mustard.

*I got it right on the test!

And I add an extra Little Betty® nut-free double oatmeal cookie, just for Franklin.

MASH-UP MADNESS!

PRINCIPAL PLANARIA + **JANITOR KALOWSKI** = **PLANOWSKI**

PEGGY + **DEE** = **PEGGY DEE**

HECTOR + **GEORGIE GIRAFFE** = **HECTIRAFFE**

NOW GO TRY DRAWING YOUR OWN MASH-UPS!

SNOOPY

IN

LUNCH TIME BEAGLE

PEANUTS CREATED BY CHARLES M. SCHULZ

ORDER IS VERY IMPORTANT TO THE HEAD BEAGLE...

grumble grumble

BUT NO ONE LIKES DAWDLERS!

LUNCH SMELLS GREAT TODAY!

MMMMM!

WE BEAGLES KNOW THAT GREAT SERVICE BEGINS WITH GREAT STYLE!

GLOP!

SPLUT!

WHAT'S THAT? A CRY FOR HELP?

WAAAH! SNOOPY, HELP!

FORTUNATELY, I AM TRAINED TO HANDLE ALL CRISES!

ZIP!

CHOMP CHOMP CHOMP CHOMP CHOMP CHOMP

YOUR TRAY WAS OVERLOADED...BUT NOT ANYMORE! NO NEED TO THANK ME!

BREAK TIME!

THE HEAD BEAGLE VALUES CLEANLINESS...

BUT WON'T CROSS THE UNIONS!

BABYMOUSE ♥

LUNCH TABLE CHAMPION

BY JENNIFER L. HOLM & MATTHEW HOLM

SOON.

HI, GANG! OUR USUAL TABLE?

OKAY!

SURE!

YEP!

LET'S DO IT!

GASP!

THIS IS **OUR** TABLE!

NOT ANYMORE.

LOOKS LIKE YOU'RE THE PEASANTS, BABYMOUSE.

SIGH.

ROBIN HOOD WAS THE
CHAMPION OF THE PEASANTS!

HE STOLE FROM THE RICH
AND GAVE TO THE POOR.

CHAMPION OF THE LUNCH TABLE!

SNAP!

OUCH!

STUPID BOW.

THE NEXT DAY AT LUNCH.

SHOVE PUSH

WHAT DO YOU THINK YOU'RE DOING?

I'M STEALING IT BACK AND GIVING IT TO THE PEASANTS. I MEAN, MY FRIENDS.

I CHALLENGE YOU FOR IT!

UH, OKAY, SURE. WHAT ARENA?

DODGEBALL.

WILT

HA! HA!

GULP.

OH, DEAR.

THANK YOU FOR JOINING MY DODGEBALL TEAM, MERRY MEN!

WE WILL TAKE BACK SHERWOOD FOREST— I MEAN, OUR LUNCH TABLE!

ANY QUESTIONS?

SLAM!

THE SUN'S IN MY EYES!

I NEED SOMETHING TO DRINK.

I DON'T WANT TO MESS UP MY HAIR!

ARE THERE TEAM SHIRTS?

BEE-ZORT SNACK?

MAYBE YOU SHOULD CALL YOURSELVES "BABYMOUSE AND HER BAND OF CRANKY DODGEBALLERS"?

SIGH.

FORSOOTH, ROBIN MOUSE.

UGH.

THE DAY OF THE CHALLENGE.

PREPARE FOR DEFEAT!

NOT LIKELY.

SHRUG

TWEET!

SWOOSH!

WHOOSH!

ZOOM!

SWISH!

WHIZZ!

BOING!

WE CAME ALL THE WAY FROM ALPHA CENTAURI TO DODGE UNIDENTIFIED FLYING OBJECTS?!

ZOOM!

FWOOSH!

WHIP!

OUCH!

MY TAIL!

THWAP!

FWACK!

MY TAIL!

HEY!

WE'RE ACTUALLY WINNING!

WHIP!

IS THAT A CUPCAKE OVER THERE?

CUPCAKE?

WHIP!

CUPCAKE?

WHIP!

I LOVE CUPCAKES!

WHIP!

CUPCAKE?

BEE-ZORT!

WHIP!

WHIP!

Little Jimmy, Kid Detective, in...

THE CASE OF THE

MISSING SCIENCE PROJECT

BY JASON SHIGA

INSTRUCTIONS

How did you get to this panel? You did it by turning the page and reading from the top like in a normal comic. But this is not a normal comic.

In this comic, you may have noticed yellow arrows connecting all the panels. The arrows can bend right, left, and even OFF the edge of a page! When that happens, follow the arrow across the edge and onto the other side.

Further in the story, arrows can even split in two or more directions. At that point YOU, the reader, can choose which branch to follow. And by making the right choices, YOU help Jimmy solve the Case of the Missing Science Project.

Oh, hello, Filbert.

Jimmy! I'm so glad I found you! You're my last hope.

Are you okay?

Aha! Your science project is a dinosaur egg. But dinosaurs are extinct.

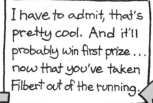
I have to admit, that's pretty cool. And it'll probably win first prize... now that you've taken Filbert out of the running.

Have a look.

Well, there's Linda. She's been my best friend since second grade.

There's Blane, the most popular kid in school.

And there's Darius. I don't know much about him other than he's not very organized.

But due to your complete lack of organization, you hadn't even started.

So you did the only logical thing you could.... You broke into Filbert's locker and used his time machine to find a dinosaur egg.

How did you get to this panel? You got here by following the yellow arrow over the edge of the previous page. But now that you have a time machine, you have the option of using it.

To use the time machine, you first must be holding the device. Then, instead of turning one page, skip over TWO pages to see where that leads you. You'll know you did it right if you see the swirly spiral.

Now flip back to the previous page and try it!

Don't thank me yet. It's broken. Right now it just takes you to a random point in time.

This is going to take an hour to fix. But presentations are in twenty minutes.

Maybe you can go to a random point yourself and fix it there.

No matter what, they couldn't play nice.

Fluent Latin speaker

KICK!

kickball champion

bounce!

Hey!

It's not my fault you don't have dodging skills!

Jock!

Sigh.

Nerd!

Washing dishes:

Stirring pots:

Serving students:

Distributing ice:

(ice)

Too much, Cullen! It will overflow!

Time for lunch break, folks! You can put that down.

Lunch Lion

Trash

Back on lunch duty:

Look! The ice is melted!

But it didn't overflow!

I wonder why not?

Well, little mice, when water FREEZES, it EXPANDS, unlike other liquids, which contract. So when ice MELTS back into water, it takes up LESS space than it did as ice. A very Successful experiment!

Cool!!

Let's try some more experiments!!

Sometimes the worst day leads to a best friend.

NOW EXTINCT, THESE TOUGH PREHISTORIC PEOPLE WERE FIERCE HUNTERS....

GRRRRRRRR

Andy, stop growling! You're scaring Tiny!

It's not me, Lucy— it's my stomach!

GRRRRR

I'm starving.

You know, eating really helps with hunger.

Ha ha, Phil.

GRRRR

That's a great idea, Phil! You can make some lunch, since everyone is getting hungry.

Hungry!

Oh, uh, sure, Mrs. Luba.

Ha! Get to work!

Maybe Lucy and Andy would like to help?

Yes, that'd be wonderful. Thank you, Phil.

Ha!

I could go for some rabbit soup... so you two have to go get a rabbit.

Why don't you go catch a rabbit.

Oh, right. You probably aren't capable of—

Yes, we are! We'll be back with a huge rabbit! Maybe a bunch of rabbits! A bunch of HUGE rabbits!

Good thing I'm with you, Lucy. It takes hunting expertise to catch a wild rabbit.

Sure, Andy.

It's not like a rabbit is just going to jump out of the bushes right in front of us.

HOP HOP HOP HOP

HOP HOP HOP

HOP HOP

chew chew chew

Andy, wait!

...because now would be a good time to use those hunting skills?

AAAAUUGGGHHH!

LATER THAT DAY

I couldn't do it....

Huff

Huff

Too fast!

I tried to tell you—we need to use strategy. Something like, you hide, and I chase the rabbit your way, then you jump on it when it gets near.

Hmmm...

Maybe I could hide, you chase the rabbit over to me, then I jump out and catch it.

That's what I said.

Not exactly.

Ready?

Ready!

Nibble Nibble

83

Shoo! Shoo!

WAAUUGGHHHH!

POUNCE!

I...I did it! Lucy, I got it! I can't believe that worked.

Don't let go!

KICK! KICK! KICK! KICK! KICK! KICK! KICK! KICK! KICK! KICK!

About time. Please tell me you caught a rabbit.

We did.

Then where is it?

We just didn't keep it.

Can't you guys do anything right?

If you can do it right, why didn't you do it?

Because you said you could help make the soup.

84

Forget about the rabbit. We'll make something else. What's your *least* favorite soup?

Pea soup. Why?

Because that's what we're having, since it's your <u>favorite</u>.

But that's our <u>LEAST</u> favorite!

So? It's still one of your favorites. Just not your <u>most</u> favorite.

Now, go pick some peas.

Why aren't you picking the good peas?

If we bring back bad ones, he'll want to make something else for lunch.

What are these? These aren't any good!

At least we didn't let them escape?

I guess we should make something else.

No, I'll send you back out with Margaret to make sure you do it right.

Margaret?

85

Margaret! Go with Lucy and Andy— they need to get peas for soup. Good peas.

Do I have to?

Hi, Margaret!

I will pick the best possible peas for you!

Ew, just don't drool on me.

How are these? Do you like them?

Sure. Looks good.

Just "good"? I can do better for you!

Sure. Looks great.

She thinks the ones I'm picking are great.

Margaret, do you want me to gather wood for the fire?

Sure, whatever.

Hey! I'm in charge here.

Andy, go get some wood.

You two get the soup together.

Hey! Why are you mixing those peas with other stuff?

It'll taste better. Did you want to take over?

No, but if it tastes bad, I'm saying you made it.

I AM Making it.

Here's the wood!

Oh, good, we can have lunch TODAY instead of NEXT WEEK.

Meat or vegetables could be boiled in animal skin.

Fire heats liquid...

NEANDERTHAL SOUP!

...but liquid keeps animal skin from catching on fire!

Keep an eye on the soup and let us know when it's ready.

You want us to just watch it until it boils?

Exactly.

Getting bossed around is boring.

Too bad we can't watch harder to make it cook faster.

Mmm, what's that smell?

Hi, Dad! Hi, Mr. Daryl!

Did you catch anything?

Da!

We tracked some deer, but didn't catch any.

Good thing there's lunch here!

Hey, you're supposed to be watching the soup!

We were watching with the backs of our heads.

Oh, no! We let it cook too long and it probably tastes HORRIBLE, Margaret.

The soup's ready, but Lucy really wanted to make it, so we let her, and I'm afraid it won't be very good.

I'm sure it's fine!

Let's just be glad we have lunch!

Why are you smiling?

So nice of Margaret to offer to clean up.

Yes.

I may take a nap.

stretch!

Don't look at me, I'm not cleaning up!

You did such a good job making the soup, Lucy, I'm sure you'll do a great job cleaning up.

It figures.

Hmmm...

What?

You guys are done cleaning up already?

No, you're done cleaning up already.

Oh, yeah, ha!

Look!

Poor Margaret didn't do a very good job cleaning up, did she?

Teenagers!

THESE LUNCHTIME STORIES ARE MAKING ME *HUNGRY*!

LISTEN TO MY TUMMY GROWL.

GGGRRRLLLLLL

IT SAID, "GIRL"!

DISGUSTING!

GIRLS AREN'T DISGUSTING. I LIKE GIRLS.

PRISONER HALE, I'VE GOT A FEELING YOU HAVE A LUNCH STORY TO ADD.

I DO.

HANG ON, DO THE READERS OF THIS BOOK KNOW WHO WE ARE?

THEY'RE *LUCKY* IF THEY DON'T KNOW WHO *YOU* ARE.

THIS IS THE AMERICAN SPY NATHAN HALE. AND WE'RE THE ONES WHO ARE GOING TO HANG HIM.

I'M THE HANGMAN.

AND I'M TIRED OF HAVING TO EXPLAIN MYSELF.

CAP'N HALE HAS SEEN ALL OF *HISTORY*--AND HE'S TELLING STORIES TO STOP US FROM HANGING HIM.

NOW, PLEASE, TELL US ABOUT SOME SORT OF HISTORICAL LUNCH.

MAKE SURE IT'S AS FUNNY AS THE OTHER STORIES IN THIS BOOK.

MUST IT BE *SILLY*? I'D LIKE A WAR STORY MYSELF.

BUT SILLY.

A LUNCH-THEMED WAR STORY THAT'S SILLY...

THAT WON'T BE EASY. WAR ISN'T SILLY.

YOU CAN DO IT, SIR. I KNOW YOU CAN.

THIS STORY TAKES PLACE IN THE SECOND WORLD WAR.

THERE'S A *SECOND* WORLD WAR?

DIDN'T THEY LEARN ANYTHING IN THE *FIRST* WORLD WAR?!

IN DECEMBER 1941, PEARL HARBOR WAS BOMBED BY JAPAN.

THE U.S. PACIFIC FLEET WAS SMASHED AND SCATTERED.

WHILE THE AMERICANS RUSHED TO REBUILD THEIR PACIFIC FLEET,

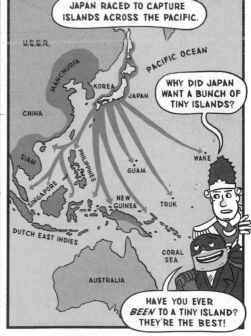

JAPAN RACED TO CAPTURE ISLANDS ACROSS THE PACIFIC.

U.S.S.R.

MANCHURIA

KOREA

JAPAN

CHINA

PACIFIC OCEAN

WHY DID JAPAN WANT A BUNCH OF TINY ISLANDS?

SIAM

PHILIPPINES

SINGAPORE

GUAM

WAKE

TRUK

NEW GUINEA

DUTCH EAST INDIES

CORAL SEA

AUSTRALIA

HAVE YOU EVER *BEEN* TO A TINY ISLAND? THEY'RE THE BEST!

HOLY MACKEREL! THIS IS COMPLEX!

WHAT DOES IT HAVE TO DO WITH LUNCH?

OBVIOUSLY, **FOOD** WAS VERY IMPORTANT TO THE SOLDIERS ON THE ISLANDS.

YES. IF SUPPLY SHIPS COULDN'T REACH THE ISLANDS, THE SOLDIERS WOULD STARVE—

BUT THAT ISN'T THE LUNCH PART OF THE STORY.

OUR STORY TAKES PLACE ABOARD A DESTROYER NAMED U.S.S. *O'BANNON*.

450

IT WAS A NEW SHIP WITH A FRESH CREW.

ON NOVEMBER 12, 1943, THEY SET OUT WITH A SQUADRON CALLED TASK GROUP 67.4.

U.S.S. CUSHING

U.S.S. LAFFEY

U.S.S. STERETT

U.S.S. O'BANNON

U.S.S. ATLANTA

U.S.S. SAN FRANCISCO

U.S.S. PORTLAND

U.S.S. HELENA

U.S.S. JUNEAU

U.S.S. AARON WARD

U.S.S. BARTON

U.S.S. MONSSEN

U.S.S. FLETCHER

IS THAT SHIP *CUSHING* NAMED AFTER A CERTAIN CIVIL WAR NAVY HERO?

IT SURE IS.

A CONVOY OF JAPANESE SHIPS IS HEADED TO GUADALCANAL ISLAND. THEY PLAN TO BOMBARD OUR AIRFIELD AND DROP OFF MORE TROOPS.

THOSE ARE *OUR* MARINES ON GUADALCANAL. WE'VE GOT TO PROTECT THEM!

WE'RE GOING TO STOP THEIR CONVOY AT THE *NEW GEORGIA SOUND*.

YOU MAY KNOW IT AS *IRON BOTTOM SOUND*.

HAHA! WHAT'S AN *IRON BOTTOM SOUND* LIKE?

IT WAS CALLED IRON BOTTOM SOUND BECAUSE SO MANY IRON SHIPS HAD BEEN SUNK THERE.

FINALLY! A REAL *FIGHTING* MISSION!

TOMORROW'S **FRIDAY** THE **13TH**. DOESN'T THAT BOTHER YOU?

NO WAY!

THERE ARE *THIRTEEN* SHIPS IN THE CONVOY.

HECK, THIRTEEN'S MY LUCKY NUMBER!

WHAT'S THE CHOW?

POTATO SOUP. PEELED 'EM MYSELF.

LOOK AT THOSE POOR GUYS ON THE USS. *FLETCHER*, THE *THIRTEENTH* SHIP IN THE LINE.

AND THEIR NUMBER, *445*, ADDS UP TO *THIRTEEN*!

LOOK AT THAT! LIGHTNING!

IT'S *SAINT ELMO'S FIRE*! OLD SAILORS SAY THAT'S A *VERY BAD OMEN*!

HOW MUCH *BAD LUCK* CAN WE GET?!

98

THE U.S.S. *O'BANNON* HAD A NEW, TOP-SECRET TECHNOLOGY ON BOARD—RADAR.

THIS ALLOWED THEM TO SEE ENEMY SHIPS APPROACHING.

IT WAS SO NEW THAT ONLY A FEW SHIPS IN TASK GROUP 67.4 HAD IT.

SIR, CONTACT! INCOMING SHIPS! THREE GROUPS!

WHAT DOES REAR ADMIRAL CALLAGHAN SAY?

WE HAVEN'T BEEN GIVEN ORDERS TO CHANGE COURSE.

ANY CLOSER AND RADAR WON'T DO US ANY GOOD.

ORDERS ARE TO GO STRAIGHT AHEAD.

HOLY SMOKES! I CAN *SEE* THEM OUT THERE. WE'RE GONNA GO RIGHT THROUGH 'EM.

SHHH.

I HOPE ADMIRAL CALLAGHAN KNOWS WHAT HE'S DOING.

WHAT *IS* HE DOING?

HARD TO PORT! *TURN!*

THE *CUSHING'S* TURNING! WE'VE GOTTA TURN TOO!

TURN! HARD TO PORT!

THE WHOLE LINE'S TURNING!

IT'S GONNA BE A *THIRTEEN-SHIP PILEUP!*

LAUNCH TORPEDO!

FLOOMP

FFFSSSSSSSSSSSSSSSSSSHHHHHHHHHH

BONK

THAT WAS A HIT! THESE TORPEDOES ARE *DUDS*!

KRAM KABLAM

450

THAT'S FRIENDLY FIRE!

THE *SAN FRANCISCO* IS FIRING ON US!

BOOM

BLAMM

THE FOLLOWING MORNING.

I TOLD YOU IT WAS AN UNLUCKY NIGHT.

WE MADE IT.

THE *FLETCHER* DIDN'T TAKE A *SCRATCH*! LUCKY THIRTEEN!

WE DID PUT A FEW SHOTS INTO THE JAPANESE FLAGSHIP.

THE FLAGSHIP'S STILL FLOATING.

NOT FOR LONG. HERE COMES THE BUZZARD BRIGADE!

B-BOOOOOM

HOLD YOUR CHEERS. WE'RE NOT SAFE *YET*!

LET'S GET OUT OF HERE! I *HATE* IRON BOTTOM SOUND!

KROOM

WHAT HAPPENED TO THE JUNEAU?!

JAPANESE SUBS!

MAKE FOR THE BASE AT ESPIRITU SANTO! AND KEEP YOUR EYES PEELED FOR MORE SUBS!

WHAT A MELEE! WHO WON?

JAPAN LOST TWO DESTROYERS AND THEIR FLAGSHIP, THE *HIEI.*

OF THE THIRTEEN AMERICAN SHIPS, ONLY THE *FLETCHER*—*LUCKY THIRTEEN*— WAS UNDAMAGED.

SIX U.S. SHIPS WERE LOST— NEARLY HALF THE GROUP.

TASK GROUP 67.4 WAS ABLE TO TURN AWAY THE JAPANESE FORCE— AT LEAST FOR A DAY.

I'D SAY THE JAPANESE WON.

YES. BUT THEIR MISSION FAILED.

JAPANESE REINFORCEMENTS DIDN'T MAKE IT TO GUADALCANAL.

YEAH, WELL, NEITHER DID AMERICAN REINFORCEMENTS. AND WE SURE COULD USE 'EM.

ARE YOU GETTING AN IDEA OF HOW DANGEROUS THE PACIFIC WAS IN WWII?

YES!

I'D SAY IT WAS *DOWNRIGHT HAZARDOUS.*

THE U.S.S. *O'BANNON* WAS SOON BACK IN IRON BOTTOM SOUND ON A BOMBARDMENT MISSION.

BOOM

I DON'T LIKE THIS PLACE—IT GIVES ME THE *HEEBIE-JEEBIES*!

IS THE ISLAND STILL THERE? WE'VE BEEN BLASTING AWAY AT IT ALL NIGHT.

AT LEAST IT DOESN'T BLAST BACK.

TATER SOUP AGAIN?

OUR SPECIALTY.

SIR, WE'VE GOT SOMETHING AHEAD.

SPOTTERS— ANYTHING?

IT'S A *SUBMARINE*— JAPANESE. LOOKS MIDSIZED. I SEE ONE DECK GUN.

THEY HAVEN'T MOVED. I DON'T THINK THEY'VE SEEN US YET.

ARE THEY ASLEEP?

IS IT A TRAP?

RAMMING SPEED. WE'RE GONNA SEND THEM STRAIGHT TO THE BOTTOM.

WE'RE NOT GOING OUT LIKE THE *JUNEAU*.

WHAT KIND OF SUB IS IT?

I DON'T KNOW.

IS IT A MINELAYER?

IT COULD BE.

IF THAT'S A MINELAYER, WE'LL BE *BLOWN TO SMITHEREENS*!

HARD TO PORT! TURN!!!

TURRRRRRRRRRNNNN!!!

!

450 450

450

BONK

HEY, COOKY, AM I HAVIN' A BAD DREAM, OR IS THAT A JAPANESE HUNTER-KILLER SUB *RIGHT NEXT TO US*!?

THAT'S A JAPANESE HUNTER-KILLER SUB RIGHT NEXT TO US.

BATTLE STATIONS!

IF THEY POINT THAT NASTY DECK GUN AT US, WE'RE DONE FOR!

WE'RE TOO CLOSE!

OUR GUNS CAN'T POINT THAT LOW!

THEY THINK WE'RE THROWING GRENADES!

I WISH THEY WERE GRENADES! THEY'RE GONNA FIGURE IT OUT IN A SECOND!

GIMME SOME O' THEM TATERS!

I AIN'T GOIN' DOWN IN IRON BOTTOM SOUND!

HARD TO STARBOARD! WITH ENOUGH DISTANCE WE CAN FIRE ON THE TOWER!

WHAT ARE THOSE BOYS ON DECK THROWING?

POTATOES, SIR.

OUR LUNCH?

WE'RE IN RANGE.

FIRE!

BLAM

THE SHIP WAS LATER GIVEN A PLAQUE:

A TRIBUTE TO THE OFFICERS AND MEN OF THE U.S.S. O'BANNON FOR THEIR INGENUITY IN USING OUR NOW PROUD POTATO TO "SINK" A JAPANESE SUBMARINE IN THE SPRING OF 1943

PRESENTED BY POTATO GROWERS OF THE STATE OF MAINE JUNE 14, 1945

WHAT AN AMAZING TALE!

I WOULDN'T EXACTLY CALL IT *SILLY,* THOUGH.

THROWING POTATOES IS SILLY. HUNDREDS OF SAILORS GOING TO A WATERY GRAVE, WELL... THAT'S NOT SO SILLY.

BUT IT'S A TRUE STORY.

IT'S A GOOD THING IT WAS *POTATO* SOUP ON THE MENU.

WHY'S THAT?

IF IT WAS *CHICKEN SOUP,* THEY'D HAVE HAD TO THROW *CHICKENS*!

BIBLIOGRAPHY

· *EYEWITNESS PACIFIC THEATER,* D. M. GIANGRECO AND JOHN T. KUEHN, STERLING, 2008

· "HORROR AT GUADALCANAL," ERNEST A. HERR, A FIRSTHAND ESSAY ON THE DESTROYER HISTORY FOUNDATION'S WEBSITE: DESTROYERHISTORY.ORG

· *ISLANDS OF HELL: THE U.S. MARINES IN THE WESTERN PACIFIC, 1944–1945,* ERIC HAMMEL, ZENITH PRESS, 2010

· *NEPTUNE'S INFERNO: THE U.S. NAVY AT GUADALCANAL,* JAMES D. HORNFISCHER, RANDOM HOUSE, 2011

· *THE PACIFIC WAR ATLAS 1941–1945,* DAVID SMURTHWAITE, FACTS ON FILE, 1995

YOU USED A BOOK CALLED *ISLANDS OF HELL* FOR A KIDS' COMIC? *SHEESH!*

Well, that kid is sitting by herself.

Is it OK if I sit here?

sniffle

WHAAAAAAAAAA!

Um . . . Don't you have a lunch?

My lunch money was stolen!

That's terrible! Here, have half of my sandwich!

Really?!

Of course!

Who took your money?

Christine did. She's so mean!

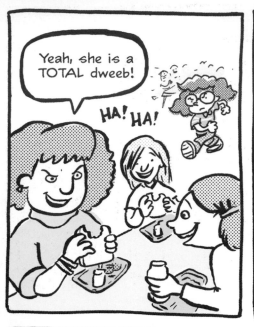

Yeah, she is a TOTAL dweeb!

HA! HA!

Christine—it was wrong of you to steal my friend's lunch money, and you should give it back!

Oh my. You're right, that was wrong. What was I thinking?! But the thing is . . .

. . . I spent all her money on this extra pudding, so . . .

Sad truth is, there are some awfully mean people in this world.

You can't let 'em get you down.

Somethin' made 'em that way.

SO yah gotta rise above!

Here are extra lunches for you and your pal!

Chin up, small fry. Justice has a way of being served.

Now you'd better head out to recess!

A few minutes later . . .

Here she comes . . .

Are you sure this is a good idea?

How could it go wrong?

Banana Peel Sliparoo

WHOOSH!

Ew. Forget her. We can't be friends with a Mud Butt!

WHAAAAA!

WHAAAAA!

The next day at lunch . . .

122

Hey, Christine . . . Maybe you might want to come over and sit with us?

sigh
No thank you. I'd rather sit here . . . all by myself.

Moldy baloney! There is no need to be alone. I'll sit with you!

Really?!

Have a seat!

SPLAT!

123

Rise above . . .

HA! HA! HA! HA! HA! HA! HA! HA! HA!

Well, thank you, Christine. I *love* chocolate!

SWISH!

WRITE YOUR OWN ORIGIN STORY!

Every hero has an origin story, and that includes **YOU**!

Make a photocopy of this page and get creative with the details!

Where do your powers come from?

How did you get to be so awesome?

Or design your own panels! Or tell your story realistically! It's your comic—it is up to **YOU**!

It was an ordinary day at _goerges school_ School . . .

But that was the day that our lunch lady served my favorite lunch, and it gave me . . .

SUPERPOWERS!

that also gave My little brother happened to my brother...

MEANWHILE

★ ABOUT THE AUTHORS ★

CECE BELL

is the author and illustrator of lots of books for kids, including the autobiographical novel *El Deafo*. She gets to eat lunch with her husband, author Tom Angleberger, practically every day. (cecebell.com)

JEFFREY BROWN

is the author of the bestselling Jedi Academy series and is currently working on his new series, Lucy & Andy Neanderthal. According to DNA testing, he is approximately 2.2% Neanderthal. (jeffreybrowncomics.com)

CECIL CASTELLUCCI & SARA VARON

are the author and illustrator of the Eisner-nominated graphic novel *Odd Duck*. Cecil is also the author of *Boy Proof*, *The Plain Janes*, and *Tin Star*. Sara's other books include *Bake Sale*, *Robot Dreams*, and *Chicken and Cat*. Like Pikput and Cullen, they both enjoy science. (misscecil.com and chickenopolis.com)

NATHAN HALE

is the author and illustrator of the Hazardous Tales series—gross and amazing true stories about history! He has also illustrated the graphic novels *Rapunzel's Revenge* and *Calamity Jack*. His favorite lunch is a huge burrito. (hazardoustales.com)

JENNIFER L. HOLM & MATTHEW HOLM

are the brother-sister team behind two graphic novel series, Babymouse and Squish. They grew up reading lots of comics, and they turned out just fine. (babymouse.com)

JARRETT J. KROSOCZKA

is the author and illustrator of the Lunch Lady graphic novel series, which chronicles the adventures of a spatula-wielding crime fighter. He has been reading and drawing comics since he was a kid, and he now has thirty books published. He has given two TED Talks and can be heard weekly on SiriusXM's Kids Place Live. (studiojjk.com)

PEANUTS

Charles M. Schulz once described himself as "born to draw comic strips." In 1950, Schulz launched his daily newspapaer comic strip, *Peanuts*, which he drew for the next fifty years. The story that appears here was created by the Schulz Studio and was written

and drawn by Vicki Scott, inked by Paige Braddock, and lettered and colored by Donna Almendrala. (Peanuts.com)

JASON SHIGA

is the author of *Meanwhile* and over twenty other comic books and graphic novels. He is also the creator of the world's second-largest interactive comic. His comics have a geeky side and often feature exciting uses of math.

Serving justice! And serving lunch!

If you liked "Cave Soup," you'll LOVE

LUCY & ANDY NEANDERTHAL

COMING SOON!